DIARY OF AN
ICE PRINCESS

Snow Place Like Home

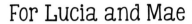

For Lucia and Mae

Copyright © 2019 by Christina Soontornvat

Illustrations by Barbara Szepesi Szucs, copyright © 2019 Scholastic Inc.

All rights reserved. Published by Scholastic Inc., *Publishers since 1920.* SCHOLASTIC and associated logos are trademarks and/or registered trademarks of Scholastic Inc.

The publisher does not have any control over and does not assume any responsibility for author or third-party websites or their content.

No part of this publication may be reproduced, stored in a retrieval system, or transmitted in any form or by any means, electronic, mechanical, photocopying, recording, or otherwise, without written permission of the publisher. For information regarding permission, write to Scholastic Inc., Attention: Permissions Department, 557 Broadway, New York, NY 10012.

This book is a work of fiction. Names, characters, places, and incidents are either the product of the author's imagination or are used fictitiously, and any resemblance to actual persons, living or dead, business establishments, events, or locales is entirely coincidental.

ISBN 978-1-338-84580-8

10 9 8 7 6 5 4 3 2 1   22 23 24 25 26

Printed in the U.S.A. 40

This edition first printing April 2022

Book design by Yaffa Jaskoll

DIARY OF AN
ICE PRINCESS

Snow Place Like Home

Christina Soontornvat

Illustrations by
Barbara Szepesi Szucs

SCHOLASTIC INC.

THE NIGHT BEFORE
THE BIG DAY

❄ FRIDAY ❄

Tonight is the perfect night to start a new diary because there is no way I can fall asleep!

Tomorrow is our family picnic. Why am I so excited, Diary? It's just a normal, old family picnic, right?

Except our picnic is in the clouds.

And our family is definitely *not* normal.

I just triple-checked all my stuff for tomorrow:

Lucky socks ✔

Lucky purple tiara ✔

Lucky dress (the only one I have that isn't ripped!) ✔

(Okay, there is a tiny rip at the shoulder and a stain on the front, but that's it!)

Normally I wouldn't be allowed to go out dressed like this. After all, I'm a princess. But Mom and Dad didn't say anything about it. I guess they know I need all the luck I can get tomorrow.

When they tucked me in tonight, they gave me a pep talk.

"Everything is going to be fine, Lina," said Dad.

"When it's time, just relax, breathe, and let the wind take you," Mom reminded me.

My mom is a Windtamer. All Windtamers have the power to control the wind and weather. Whenever she wants to go somewhere, she just waves her hand and calls up a gust of wind. The wind holds her up and carries her wherever she tells it to go.

My dad is a Groundling. In other words: human. He's a pilot, and he met my mom during a rainstorm (that she made!). She rescued him, and the rest is history.

Dad and my dog, Gusty, always ride to the picnic with Mom. They have to, or else they'd fall straight out of the sky and go *splat!*

I ride with Mom, too, because I'm still learning. But soon I'll be able to fly all by myself using my own magic.

I'm a Windtamer, just like Mom. I can control the wind. Well, not so much control the wind as ask it to

do what I want. Sometimes it listens.
Sometimes it . . .

Nope, not going to think about that
right now!

Everything is going to be just perfect.

TO THE CASTLE OF
THE NORTH WIND

☀ SATURDAY ☀

Well, Diary, everything *started* perfect.

We stepped outside our castle
and Mom called up the wind. The air
swirled under Gusty and me and picked
us up, up, up!

"Everyone ready?" shouted Mom.

"Ready!" I shouted back.

(When you travel by wind, you do a lot of shouting.)

Off we went, swooping over the clouds. Soon our palace was far behind us and we were zipping north. When I looked down, I saw rivers and forests and mountains. My favorite things to look at from above are towns. All the buildings look like dollhouses, and I love imagining all the cool, exciting stuff everyone is doing down there.

"Okay, Lina, it's almost time!" Mom shouted.

I told myself there was no reason to be nervous.

Because when I get nervous, things go wrong.

But as soon as we got in sight of Granddad's castle, I got nervous.

Because my granddad is not some normal, old granddad, Diary.

My granddad is the North Wind.

3

A COOL ENTRANCE

The North Wind.

Boreas.

General of the Wind.

Those are just some of the names
humans have given him over the years.
(Granddad has been around a really long
time.)

People all over the world tell different stories about him:

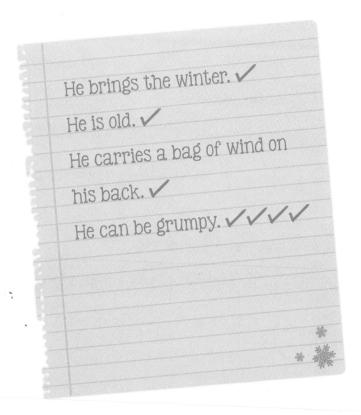

He brings the winter. ✔

He is old. ✔

He carries a bag of wind on his back. ✔

He can be grumpy. ✔✔✔✔

Granddad says I'm his favorite, but he's always nagging me to practice my powers more. Well, this time, I was ready to show him that I really could do it!

When I thought more about seeing my family, I got excited. I imagined them watching me fly into the castle all by myself. I imagined they would cheer. Some of them would be so proud, they might even cry a little.

"Okay, Lina, you got this!" Mom shouted when we got to his castle. "I'm giving control of the wind to you now!"

I concentrated on the gust of air under my feet. I was doing it! I was in control!

That's when the castle doors burst

open, and—

"IT'S ABOUT TIME MY FAVORITE

GRANDDAUGHTER SHOWED UP!"

(That's how Granddad talks. He yells.)

Behind him, I saw my entire family,

waiting for us, staring at me.

And then I froze. *Literally.*

When I get nervous, my wind powers go out of whack and things can get icy.

The current of air I was riding suddenly turned into an ice sheet.

My feet slipped out from under me and I went sliding!

That might have been a cool way to make an entrance, but I slid right into Granddad, who fell on top of Great-Aunt Eastia, who tumbled on top of Cousin Rodney, who toppled the dessert table.

"LINA!" boomed Granddad. "WHAT DO YOU HAVE TO SAY FOR YOURSELF?"

I looked at him. I looked at my family. And I said, "Um, is there any ice cream cake left?"

4

FAMILY SECRETS

I didn't exactly make the entrance I was dreaming of. But my family was still happy to see me.

The rest of the day was a lot of fun. I played cards with my cousins. Rodney always tries to cheat, but this time we didn't let him.

OUR FAMILY ALBUM

ME

MOM
Princess Gail, brings the spring rain, makes the best noodle soup ever

DAD
Henry Rudder, daredevil, loves movies, makes us all laugh

GRANDDAD
Likes to shout, rules the skies, loves ice cream cake

COUSIN RODNEY
Plays annoying tricks, like shocking you when you shake hands

COUSIN HAILEY
Texts her boyfriend, loves extreme sports and extreme weather

GREAT-AUNT SUNDER
Not here. No one talks about her. Ever.

GREAT-UNCLE WESTON
Peppermints in his pocket, makes the perfect summer breeze

GREAT-AUNT EASTIA
Glasses, wagging finger, tells me I need to act more princess like

My other cousin, Hailey, gave me a cool silver streak in my hair. Great-Aunt Eastia made her famous mango-and-whipped-cloud pudding. It's probably my favorite thing to eat in the whole sky.

I love my family, but I wish I had some more cousins my own age. I'm usually the only kid.

When we were getting ready to leave, I heard Mom talking to Granddad. I think they were trying to have a private chat, but Granddad is no good at keeping quiet.

Granddad: "WHEN I WAS HER AGE, I-"

Mom: "Already had control of your powers. I know, Dad. You say it every year."

Granddad: "WELL, IT'S TRUE! AND LINA SHOULD LEARN TO CONTROL HER POWERS TOO. I CAN TEACH HER EVERYTHING SHE NEEDS TO KNOW."

Mom: "Lina has been practicing. She just moves at her own pace, that's all."

Granddad: "YOU NEED TO MOVE
YOUR FAMILY UP HERE WITH ME. WE'VE
ALREADY WASTED VALUABLE TIME."

When I heard that, I stopped
listening. My stomach did a barrel roll.
Move in with Granddad? Live in his
freezing-cold castle, way up north?

I love my Granddad, Diary, but I do
not want to move.

Not even if we ate mango-and-
whipped-cloud pudding every day.

5

THE ROYAL FAMILY HITS THE BEACH

☀ SUNDAY ☀

Diary, I think Mom and Dad knew I was bummed out because this morning they told me something they knew would cheer me up:

"Lina, pack your stuff—we're going down to the beach!"

When I heard that, all my thoughts about Granddad and moving vanished.

My dad grew up in a little house (lucky) right on the beach (super lucky). I love everything about it.

But the best thing about going to the beach is that my best friend lives there.

(Okay, Claudia is my *only* friend, but she's still the best.)

Claudia knows about me being a princess and a Windtamer. I had to tell her when her kitten got stuck in a tree and Mom had to use her powers to get it down. But she still treats me like I'm completely normal. When I'm with her,

I *feel* normal, like a regular kid. No one fusses after me or tells me to act more like a princess. No one reminds me to practice my powers. I can just be me.

When Claudia saw me, she squealed, "LINAAAAAAAA!"

And we did our super-secret best friend dance.

Mom used her powers to create the best boogie-boarding waves. We rode them for hours, until the sun started to go down and our fingers were as wrinkled as dried plums.

Later I told Claudia everything about my granddad, and how he wants me to go study with him.

"The worst thing is that if we move, I'll spend even less time with you," I grumbled.

"Maybe not." Claudia got that look in her eye. That *I-have-a-plan* look. "You said your family can move anywhere in the world, right?"

That *is* true, Diary. Our cloud palace

can float anywhere in the sky Mom tells
it to go.

"But my parents wouldn't move us
somewhere for no reason," I told her.

Claudia's eyes twinkled. "I think I
have the perfect reason. I'll show you.
Tomorrow morning. My house."

CLAUDIA'S PERFECT PLAN

❋ MONDAY ❋

I raced to Claudia's house as soon as I woke up this morning. In her room, she showed me a stack of papers:

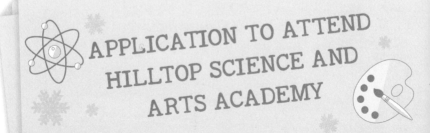

APPLICATION TO ATTEND HILLTOP SCIENCE AND ARTS ACADEMY

I was confused. "You want me to apply to your school? I can't do that. I don't live here."

"That doesn't matter," said Claudia. "It's a magnet school."

"You mean all the kids stick to the walls?"

"No!" She laughed. "It just means that they have special science classes. Anyone can go there. They just have to apply."

"I *am* really good at science . . ." I said.

"Exactly! If you get accepted, then maybe you can convince your parents you don't need to move in with your grandfather. We could go to the same school!"

I imagined what that would be like:

It was worth a try, Diary.

So I went for it!

Now the question is: Will Mom and Dad go for it too?

7

BIG PROMISES

✳ WEDNESDAY ✳

Things I'm good at:

✳ Science

✳ Boogie boarding

✳ Teaching Gusty tricks

Things I'm not so good at:

* Knowing when the mail will arrive

"LINA!"

I guess Mom can shout as loud as Granddad when she wants to.

I ran downstairs. Mom waved a piece of paper and scowled. The paper said:

CONGRATULATIONS!

You have been accepted to Hilltop Science and Arts Academy.

Diary, I got in!

Happy dance! Fist pumping! Woo-hoo!

Mom was not as happy. "A *Groundling* school? Lina, what were you thinking?"

I explained everything: how I didn't want to live with Granddad all the time, how lonely I was, and how this was my one chance to be just like all the other kids.

"But you're not like the other kids," said Mom. "You're a princess. A Windtamer."

Dad came downstairs. He and Mom went into their room to "discuss the matter." It wasn't looking good. Gusty came over and nuzzled his head into my lap.

That gave me an idea. When I was little, Mom and Dad had wanted me to get a pet bird. They said it would be easier to take care of a bird in our cloud palace.

But I wanted a dog so bad! So I made a list of all the things I promised to do to take care of Gusty. It showed them how responsible I could be.

I decided to make a list for Groundling school.

Dear Mom and Dad, if you let me go to Hilltop Academy, I promise to:

1. Do my homework every night

2. Pack my own lunch

3. Not let anyone at school know I'm a princess or a Windtamer, ever

I slid the note under Mom and Dad's door. I waited. The door opened.

Mom and Dad looked down at my note. They looked at each other.

Mom sighed. "Lina, we have decided to give this Groundling school a try . . ."

I jumped in the air!

". . . as long as you keep these promises you made . . ."

I jumped some more!

". . . and as long as you spend every Saturday studying with your grandfather."

I quit jumping.

Mom put her hands on my shoulders. "We know this school is important to you. But your powers are important to the *whole sky*. You can't neglect your duties as a princess. So do we have a deal?"

I thought about it for two nanoseconds. "It's a deal!"

Next week, Diary.

I am going to a regular school next week.

On the *ground*.

8

GROUNDLING SCHOOL

* MONDAY *

Diary, I was so excited for the first day of school, I could hardly sleep last night! Mom and Dad got me this cool thing called a *backpack*. It's a pack for your back! And we filled it with all the incredible things I'd need for class.

Mom had a lot of work to do in the Southern Hemisphere, so Dad dropped me off at school the first day. He landed his plane in a field nearby. Before we got out to walk to school, he handed me a bag. Inside were . . . clothes.

"But I picked out my best dress just for today!"

"Honey, as much as I love that gown, I think this might be more appropriate to wear to Groundling school. Take it from an actual Groundling."

Dad gave me a big, long hug before I went inside. "I'm proud of you, Lina. I hope your first day goes great."

How could it not, Diary?!

9

THAT DARN AIR-CONDITIONING

Our teacher's name is Ms. Collier. I knew right away I was going to love her.

Ms. Collier had everyone play some get-to-know-you games. Then we organized all our school supplies and labeled our folders. Then we went over

our weekly schedule and made a "Class Contract."

I couldn't believe it. It was all so *normal*. It was exactly what I'd been dreaming of.

It was the very best day of my life.

At least it *was*, until after lunch.

In the afternoon, the classroom started to get a little hot. Ms. Collier opened the windows, but everyone was still sweating.

"We need a breeze in here!" she said.

I don't know what I was I thinking. I guess the truth is, I wasn't thinking much at all.

I just knew that I really liked Ms. Collier and I wanted to make her happy. So I thought I could use my powers to create a gentle breeze.

No big deal. Just a teensy bit of wind.

The breeze I made was perfect.

"Ah, that's much better," said Ms. Collier.

But a few minutes later, the boy

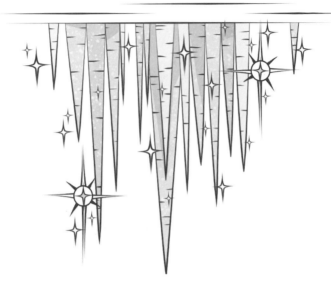

sitting next to me said, "Hey, something just dripped on my nose!"

Drip! Drip! I felt it too.

Claudia tapped my shoulder. "Lina, look up!"

Oh. My. Glaciers.

Icicles. Gigantic, glittering icicles hung down from the ceiling.

I started to freak out, which only

made things worse. The classroom got colder. The icicles grew bigger. Specks of frost swirled in the air.

Then everyone else started to freak out.

Ms. Collier clapped her hands. "Class, class! Calm down! I'm sure there is a logical explanation for . . . icicles on the ceiling?"

Claudia stood up. "It's the air-conditioning! It happens at my house *all* the time! Me and Lina will go tell the office to call the janitor!"

Claudia pulled me out the door and into the hall. "Lina, did you do that?"

"I guess so! I don't know!"

But I did know. Of course it was me. Who else would it be?

I felt horrible, but I knew I needed to calm down. We went to the office. They called the janitor and he unfroze the ceiling with a hair dryer.

From now on, Diary, I am never going to try to use my powers at school again.

Maybe Groundling school isn't going to be as breezy as I thought!

10

THE WAY OF THE WIND

SATURDAY

Well, Diary, the first week of Groundling

school was a little unexpected.

But today is Saturday, so I knew

exactly what to expect when I got to

Granddad's castle.

Shouting.

"LINA! YOU'RE LATE AGAIN! WE'VE ALREADY LOST VALUABLE TIME!"

Granddad's castle is cold and enormous. It has hundreds of rooms, which would be awesome to play hide-and-seek in with Gusty. But we weren't there to play.

In the library, Granddad handed me a fluffy, white dandelion. **"TIME FOR YOUR FIRST CHALLENGE."**

I took a big breath and started to blow . . .

"NO, NO, NO! USE YOUR POWERS!"

I stared at the dandelion. I thought blustery, gustery, windy thoughts. I concentrated with all my might.

Finally I was able to create a puff
of air that blew the seeds off! I
was so proud. I was also *so* tired!
I thought I'd get to rest or maybe get a
snack, but–

   "FOLLOW ME! TIME FOR YOUR NEXT
CHALLENGE!"

   We worked *all* morning.

Granddad was teaching me what he called "The Way of the Wind."

"THERE IS A WIND IN YOUR HEART. IF YOU LISTEN TO YOUR HEART, THE WIND WILL LISTEN TO YOUR COMMAND."

I closed my eyes and thought really commanding thoughts. But the best I could ever do was create a light breeze. At least I didn't make it snow!

By the afternoon I was huffing and puffing.

"Granddad, I think I'm good. I got this Windtamer stuff down. Don't you think we could call it a day?"

"LINA, LET ME SHOW YOU WHAT WE ARE WORKING TOWARD."

Granddad took me outside to the castle courtyard. Every tower of his castle has a small statue of a wind dragon perched on top. One of the statues had tumbled off and lay in the middle of the courtyard.

"BY THE TIME WE'RE DONE WITH YOUR LESSONS, YOU WILL USE YOUR MAGIC TO LIFT THAT STATUE BACK TO ITS PROPER PLACE."

I gulped. The statue looked heavy. The tower looked high.

"Um, what if I can't do it?"

Granddad waggled his very bushy eyebrows at me.

"THEN YOU WILL SPEND MORE TIME PRACTICING!"

I know what that means, Diary. More time practicing means less time at Groundling school. If I want to stay at Hilltop Academy, I have to figure out how to put that statue back.

TEENSY TINY PROBLEMS

✳ MONDAY ✳

I can't imagine ever leaving Hilltop
Academy. I love it more every day.

Ms. Collier is the best teacher I've
ever had. (Okay, she's the only teacher
I've ever had, but she's still awesome!).
Right now we're learning about solids,

✳ 55 ✳

liquids, and gases. Ms. Collier showed us

how to make this goopy substance:

RECIPE FOR GOOP

1 cup water

2 cups cornstarch

Combine and stir.

Goop is runny like a liquid, but when you

squeeze it, it's solid!

What is this stuff?

At the end of the month, we have the

science fair, which is where everyone does

a science project and presents it to a group

of judges. The best projects win ribbons.

Claudia and I are going to do an

experiment with soda and candy
that she read about on the internet.
(Yummiest experiment ever!) Claudia
wins a ribbon every year, and this year
we know we'll get first place.

Besides science, there are other
amazing things about Groundling school.
There's PE, where we get to do all sorts
of fun stuff I never do in the clouds.

In music class, we're learning to play different instruments. Our teacher, Mr. Bennett, loves rock 'n' roll, and he's teaching us how to rock out.

I wish I could say that the icicles were my only magical disaster, but the truth is that I've had a couple of teensy tiny slipups.

* Froze the water fountain

* Frosted over the windows in the cafeteria

* Turned the boys' bathroom into an ice-skating rink

I don't understand! After the
icicle fiasco, I haven't been using my
Windtamer powers at all. Why does
my magic keep going wacky when I'm
not even trying to use it?

I wonder if I should ask Mom
what's going on. But I'm supposed to be
keeping my powers a secret. If she finds

out my magic is messing up on its own, she'll take me out of school.

No, Diary. I'll just have to keep everything cool—Ack!

Not *cool*.

Warm. That's it. *Warm*.

Everything is totally warm and under control.

12

FREEZE TAG

✷ WEDNESDAY ✷

Today everything went completely out of control.

I was trying *so hard* not to think about ice, or snow, or cold. But somehow I slipped up.

Again.

It was all because of a kid named Dylan.

SPIKY HAIR

LOTS OF KEY CHAINS ON HIS BACKPACK

FANCY, FAST SNEAKERS

Dylan is the best runner in our class. He wins every race in PE. The kid is fast. And he knows it.

Today we were playing tag at recess, and Dylan kept saying, "If anyone can tag me, I'll give them a thousand dollars!"

When it was my turn to be "it," I made a decision. Even though I don't have that much experience with ground running, I was going to tag him out.

Dylan took off across the soccer field. I chased after him. He ran faster. I put my head down and ran as fast as I could . . .

"Tag!"

I actually caught him!

"Okay, Dylan, where's my thousand dollars?" I said.

Dylan looked shocked. Then he looked mad. "You didn't *actually* tag me. You just touched my shirt. It doesn't count."

What? I'd tagged him fair and square, on the shoulder!

Dylan started to run off.

"Stop!" I shouted. He was cheating! I was so angry.

The weird thing was: He did stop. And that's when I realized that Dylan's fancy, fast sneakers were frozen to the ground in solid blocks of ice.

Dylan twisted and pulled, but he was stuck tight. "Hey, what's going on? I can't move!"

I didn't know what to do, so I ran to find Claudia.

"You mean, you *literally* froze him in freeze tag?" she said.

"Um, maybe?"

"Lina! What are you going to do?"

"Well, the sun is out, so he'll probably melt in a few minutes, but . . ."

Claudia gave me a look. It was a *quit-dodging-the-question* look. "I mean, what are you going to do about all this ice stuff? Do your mom and dad know what's going on?"

"Not exactly . . ."

Out on the soccer field, Dylan's ice blocks were melting into a muddy puddle. "My sneakers are getting dirty!" he whined.

"The science fair is in a week!" Claudia said. "Promise me you won't get in trouble or mess anything else up before then. We *have* to win!"

I held out my pinkie to her. "Everything is going to be fine. I promise."

I have never broken a pinkie promise to Claudia, Diary. I'm not going to start now.

13

THE HALL OF ANCESTORS

✷ SATURDAY ✷

I wish I could quit freezing stuff, Diary!

I wish Claudia and I could win first place in the science fair.

I wish I could sleep late on Saturdays.

But I'm a wind princess, not a wish

princess, so you can guess where I had to go this morning.

"LISTEN TO YOUR HEART! FOCUS ON WHAT YOU'RE DOING!"

I stared at the dragon statue so hard my eyeballs almost popped out.

"NOT SO TENSE! YOU'VE GOT TO RELAX!"

I let my arms go wiggly like noodles.

"LINA, STOP GOOFING AROUND! YOU'VE GOT TO TAKE THIS SERIOUSLY!"

Couldn't Granddad see how seriously I was taking it?

"I AM *TRYING!*"

Whoa. I yelled. At Granddad. Nobody yells at Granddad.

I stared at him. He stared at me. I waited for him to shout back.

Instead, he took a deep breath. "You're right, Lina, you are trying. I think it's time I showed you something important."

"Is it another challenge?"

"Not quite. NOW FOLLOW ME!"

(The quiet talking was nice while it lasted.)

I followed Granddad to a part of his castle I've never visited before: a long hallway with pictures covering the walls.

"LINA, THIS IS THE HALL OF ANCESTORS."

Wow. Mom had told me about some of my ancestors. They were our family members from long ago. But I had never seen their pictures before.

There was even a picture of me, as a baby with my mom and dad.

When I saw that, it hit me: Being a Windtamer was a really big deal, and I

THE WINDTAMER-
RUDDER FAMILY

GREAT-GREAT-GREAT-
GRANDMOTHER SAMYA

COUSIN
HAILEY

GRANDDAD

GREAT-GREAT-UNCLE
VINCENT

was a part of it. I felt a funny tingle up and down my arms.

"Wow, Granddad, this is really amazing."

"THIS IS WHERE YOUR MAGIC COMES FROM, LINA. THIS IS YOUR FAMILY. I KNOW I CAN BE HARD ON YOU. BUT IT'S BECAUSE I KNOW YOU'RE SPECIAL. IT'S UP TO YOU TO CARRY ON OUR FAMILY LINE. ONE DAY YOU WILL DO INCREDIBLE THINGS, JUST LIKE ALL YOUR ANCESTORS BEFORE YOU."

I think I understand Granddad now, Diary. He loves me very much. All the shouting and the nagging is just his way of showing me that.

Mom had told me it was important to learn how to be a Windtamer, but I didn't really get it until now.

The whole sky is depending on me.

14

STAY WARM

FRIDAY

Diary, today was the big day. The
science fair.

We had everything ready for our
Candy and Soda Explosion Experiment.
I stayed up late finishing our poster.

Claudia had run the experiment over and over in her backyard until it was perfect. This is how it was supposed to work:

The cold soda fizzes a little bit. The warm soda makes a GIGANTIC explosion!

I could tell Claudia was really nervous. That made *me* nervous.

I told myself to be calm, but I couldn't stop thinking about all the other times I had messed things up. Claudia was depending on me. *Everyone* was depending on me.

"Stay warm," I told myself. "Stay warm . . ."

It was our turn to show our demonstration. The judges gathered near. Claudia dropped the mint candy into the cold soda bottle. It fizzed a little bit. Then she dropped the candy into the warm soda bottle, and . . .

. . . nothing happened.

The judges looked confused.

That's when I saw it. Ice on the soda bottle. Claudia saw it too. Our big explosion wouldn't work unless the soda was warm.

"Can you explain what's going on?" one of the judges asked.

In the science fair, it's okay if your experiment doesn't go right, as long as you can explain in your own words what happened. Claudia looked at me. Of course she couldn't explain what happened.

Because *I'm* what happened. I ruined everything.

Claudia looked devastated.

I had broken my promise to her. I had let her down.

I heard someone in the gym shout, "Oh my gosh, you guys, look out the window!"

Outside, the sky was white.

Snow. Big, fat, swirling flakes of snow.

My sadness turned to panic. I had made it snow. In September.

I tried to stop it. I focused. I did everything Granddad told me to. But the air got colder, and the snow swirled harder.

The teachers opened the gym doors and . . . a *gigantic* snowdrift flowed right into the gym.

Our principal got on the loudspeaker: "The science fair is ended for the day! We are going to have early dismissal due to . . . this crazy weather!"

Everyone in the gym cheered.

Everyone except for Claudia and me, Diary. What had I done?

15

DOGS KNOW BEST

The newspapers call it "the Blizzard of the Century."

I call it the worst day of my life, Diary.

We didn't earn a ribbon in the science fair. Not even honorable mention.

Claudia says she isn't mad at me. But she didn't talk to me much yesterday. She didn't really talk to anyone. I can tell she's upset.

And why shouldn't she be?

I ruined the whole project. I let my best friend down.

I let myself down.

Gusty keeps whining and nuzzling his head into my lap.

I wish Gusty could talk. I think he wishes that too. I guess he knows I need to talk to someone.

You know what?

Sometimes you have to listen to your dog.

16

PRINCESS TO PRINCESS

Mom has a really big job. She brings the spring rains to people all over the world. She's almost always busy, even early on Saturday mornings.

When I asked her to talk, I expected her to tell me to wait until later.

But she put her work down. "Of course, sweetie. What is it?"

"I don't know if I should tell you. This is pretty . . . um, serious."

Mom put her arm around my shoulder and pulled me close. "Lina, you can tell me anything. No matter how serious it is, I'll love you and support you. Pinkie promise."

We shook pinkies. And then I told her everything.

The icicles, the water fountain, the freeze tag, the Blizzard of the Century. All of it.

She hugged me really tight. "Lina, I'm so glad you told me all this."

"I just wanted to be like everyone
else at school."

"Oh, sweetheart, you *aren't* like
everyone else at school . . ."

I knew what was coming. I'd have to
leave Groundling school. I'd have to go
live with Granddad.

". . . and you aren't like anyone in the sky either."

Huh?

She smiled. "You are *you*, Lina. And that is a wonderful, magical thing."

"But–but what about Granddad? And being a Windtamer? I'm going to let down our ancestors!"

"Your grandfather loves you for you too. And I'll talk to him about all the Windtamer stuff. Maybe it's time to take a little break."

"Mom?" I took a deep breath and asked, "Does this mean I can't go to school with Claudia anymore?"

Mom took an even deeper breath and nodded. "Maybe it's time to take a little break from Hilltop Academy too. At least until we can figure out what's going on with your powers."

I wanted to argue, but I knew she was right. It was still a crummy thing to hear.

Mom hugged me extra, super tight. "We are going to figure this out as a family. But for now, your grandfather is expecting us. Gusty, you're coming too, buddy!"

I still felt sad about the science fair. And I felt crushed about having to take time off from school. But I also felt a

thousand times better not having that
big secret hanging over me anymore.

I've got the smartest dog in the
whole sky. (Okay, he's the *only* dog in the
sky, but he's still awesome.)

17

NOT A MISTAKE

When we got to Granddad's castle, Mom
went to talk to him alone. I didn't hear
any shouting, which I thought was a
good sign.

I sat at the bottom of the stairs,
thinking about what Mom had said.

If I wasn't like the other kids, and I wasn't like Granddad, then who was I supposed to be?

I remembered all the times I had made ice or snow at school.

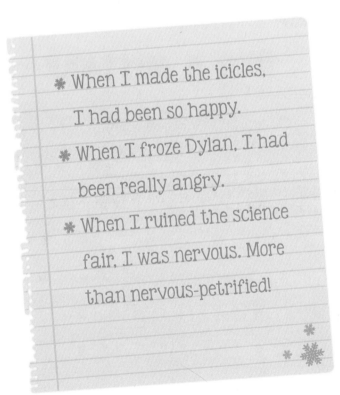

* When I made the icicles, I had been so happy.
* When I froze Dylan, I had been really angry.
* When I ruined the science fair, I was nervous. More than nervous-petrified!

I realized that every time my magic messed up, I had been feeling something really strong.

What if all that ice and snow wasn't a mistake? What if it was . . . me?

I shut my eyes and did what Granddad taught me. I focused. But not too hard. I listened to my heart.

And then I opened my eyes.

All around me, the air was full of tiny snowflakes! They weren't falling. They were just hanging out in the air. I could see every pattern. Each one was different and beautiful in its own way.

"Mom! Granddad! You have to see this!"

I ran down the hall to find them.
I stopped when I got to the castle
courtyard.

There was something I had to do
first.

18

THE BIG TEST

The statue of the wind dragon stared at me with its stone eyes.

It still looked heavy. And the tower still looked high.

I took a deep breath.

The snowflakes formed again in the

air all around me. They were beautiful,
and I had made them!

I felt so proud and happy. Everything
felt *right*.

I waved my hand, and the snow
gathered and swooped. I swished my
arm to the side and the snow followed!

I got nervous for a second. What if

the snow got out of hand? What if I lost control?

Then I reminded myself that I didn't need to be afraid. The snow wasn't a mistake.

It was *me*.

I twirled my hands, forming the snow into a big white swirl. The snow curled around and around the tower. Soon a glittering ramp of snow ran all the way from the ground to the tower roof.

Gusty barked and jumped.

"All right, buddy. I know you want to help. Let's do this together!"

I twirled my fingers to make a block of ice. I formed it into a sled. Then I tied Gusty up to the front. I heaved the dragon statue onto the back of the sled.

"Okay, Gusty, let's go!"

Together we ran up the snow ramp, around and around the tower. It was easy for Gusty to pull the ice sled. He wasn't even tired by the time we got to the top. I heaved the dragon statue back into its proper place.

Mom rushed outside. "Lina!"

"LINA!" (Granddad was right behind.)

They looked up and saw me at the top of the tower. I had done it, Diary. I completed Granddad's challenge!

I scooped up Gusty and put him beside me on the sled. We slid down, down

the snow ramp all the way to the
ground.

When I got to the bottom, Mom
grabbed me and hugged me tight.

Granddad waggled his bushy
eyebrows at me.

"Granddad, I know this isn't exactly
what you had in mind, but–"

"LINA, YOU DID NOT USE THE WIND BECAUSE YOU ARE NOT A WINDTAMER . . ."

I gulped.

". . . YOU ARE A WINTERHEART!"

A CHANGE OF HEART

A Winterheart?

That's what I am, Diary. A Winterheart!

I have my own powers, and they all involve ice and snow.

Granddad explained to me that most of

our family are Windtamers, but some of us have different types of magic:

WINDTAMERS CONTROL THE
WIND AND THE WEATHER

STORMSTIRRERS MAKE BIG
STORMS, LIKE HURRICANES
AND TORNADOES

SPARKARCHERS CREATE
LIGHTNING AND THUNDER

SKYPAINTERS MAKE SUNSETS
AND RAINBOWS

WINTERHEARTS CONTROL
SNOW AND ICE

"Is anyone else in our family a Winterheart?" I asked.

Granddad gave Mom a funny look. He changed the subject.

"YOU HAVE MADE ME PROUD, LINA. YOU PASSED YOUR TEST. YOU CAN CONTROL YOUR POWERS, EVEN

THOUGH THEY AREN'T THE ONES
I THOUGHT YOU HAD."

"Mom, does this mean I can keep going to Groundling school?" I asked.

She smiled. "I think that's exactly what it means."

"Mom! Thank you!"

I hugged her tighter than I ever have before. Then I turned to Granddad.

"Granddad, I think I still need to practice my magic. Can I still come here on Saturdays and work with you?"

"YOU WOULD REALLY WANT THAT?"

"Of course! Well, as long as I can sleep in a little."

"GRANDDAUGHTER, YOU HAVE A DEAL. I HATE WAKING UP EARLY ON SATURDAYS!"

Just to make sure, I made him pinkie promise me.

Wow, Diary, it feels amazing to have passed Granddad's test, and to finally know who I really am.

Now there's just one more person I need to talk to.

20

CLAUDIA'S EVEN-MORE-PERFECT PLAN

☀ SUNDAY ☀

I worried that Claudia wouldn't
understand. I worried she'd still be mad
at me for ruining the science fair. But
she's my best friend, and I didn't want
to keep a secret from her.

After I told her everything, she said, "I don't get it . . . you *love* the beach."

I shrugged. "I still love it. I just can't make those perfect boogie-boarding waves."

"But you *could* make us snow cones?"

"Claudia, I could make you so many snow cones, you'd have brain freeze for a year."

"That. Is. So. AWESOME!"

We hugged each other. And then we did our super-secret best friend dance. We even added a new move!

"I am really bummed that we didn't win anything in the science fair," I said.

"That's okay," said Claudia. "We know our experiment worked, even though no one else did. Hey, wait a second . . ."

Claudia got that look on her face. That *I-have-a-plan* look.

"What if we could do our experiment again, but do it even bigger and better than ever?"

"You mean like another science fair?" I asked.

"Not the science fair. I'm talking about something else . . ."

21

LISTEN TO YOUR HEART

FRIDAY

The only thing more awesome than

candy + soda + explosions

is

candy + soda + explosions + rock 'n' roll!

Claudia and I were the last ones to perform at the Hilltop Talent Show. Everyone was there. Ms. Collier, Mr. Bennett, Mom and Dad, Claudia's family.

"Okay, we've got everything set up," said Claudia from backstage. "Are you ready?"

I gave her the thumbs-up. The curtain rose.

Our rock 'n' roll song played over the speakers. Right on cue, Claudia and I dropped the candies into the soda bottles.

She looked at me. I think she wondered if I could really keep my powers under control. But the bottles stayed warm.

And the soda . . .

EXPLODED!

In time to the music!

Everyone in the audience jumped to their feet and cheered.

We weren't done yet.

I stepped behind the stage curtain so no one could see me. I waved my hands over the auditorium. The soda droplets froze into tiny, perfect, sweet crystals. I had made sodaflakes.

They floated down slowly, over the crowd.

Everyone caught them on their tongues.

Mom and Dad gave me a thumbs-up.

Claudia and I high-fived.

The janitor scratched his head. "What is up with this air-conditioning?"

It was the best rock 'n' roll science sodaflake show in the history of the world. (Okay, it was the *only* one, but it was still completely amazing.)

THE END

Make Ms. Collier's Mystery Goop!

Is it a liquid, a solid—or something else?

YOU WILL NEED:

* A large mixing bowl

* 2 cups cornstarch + a little extra

* 1 cup water

MIX IT UP!

Measure 2 cups of cornstarch into the mixing bowl. Slowly add water until the mixture thickens. It should flow like a liquid when you tilt the bowl, but stiffen up when you squeeze it between your fingers. If it's too runny, add more cornstarch.

TRY THIS:

Scoop up a handful of the goop and let it sit in your hand. Does it run through your fingers? Now squeeze it into your fist. Does it harden into a ball? Explore this strange stuff some more, and then decide what you think: Is it a liquid or a solid?

SO WHAT IS UP WITH THIS STUFF?

The behavior of this goop depends on how much *force* you put on it (like when you squeeze or press it). The more force you apply, the thicker—and more solid-like—the goop gets. But if you touch it softly or let it sit in your fingers, the goop acts like a liquid.

The technical term for this funky stuff is *non-Newtonian fluid*, which basically means that it doesn't act like other common liquids, like water. Other non-Newtonian fluids include ketchup and quicksand!

Be cool–not warm–and read a sneak peek of Lina's next adventure!

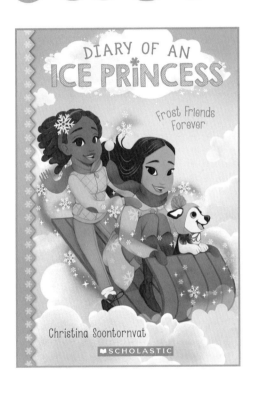

Bring on the Break

WEDNESDAY

Dear Diary,

This weekend is the start of Hilltop Science and Arts Academy's winter break, and I have to say I'm pretty excited.

Don't get me wrong, I love school. What's not to love?

My best friend, Claudia, sits next to me in class. ✔

Ms. Collier is the coolest teacher ever. ✔

I get to be a regular kid, and no one knows I'm actually a princess. ✔

But even though school is awesome, I'm looking forward to having no homework for a little while. Ms. Collier did give us one assignment, but it actually sounds fun.

"Class, I want you all to keep a Science Observation Notebook over the break," she told us this morning. "Whenever you notice science in action, write it down in your notebook. It can be anything we've learned about in class: animals, moving objects, weather . . ."

CHRISTINA SOONTORNVAT grew up behind the counter of her parents' Thai restaurant, reading stories. These days she loves to make up her own, especially if they involve magic. Christina also loves science and worked in a science museum for years before pursuing her dream of being an author. She still enjoys cooking up science experiments at home with her two young daughters. You can learn more about Christina and her books on her website at soontornvat.com.

Oh my glaciers, Diary!

Princess Lina is the *coolest* girl in school!